My goldfish never moans
She never says,
"Don't climb that tree."

She never tells me,
"Don't throw stones."

But Mum just moans
and moans and moans.

Don't dig holes.
Don't pick that rose.

Don't untie your sister's bows.

Hang that coat up.
Dry that bowl.

Don't mix jam with soap and coal.

Come on, slowcoach, hurry up.

Eat that toast.
Don't drop that cup.

Fold those clothes up.
Blow your nose.

Did you dry between your toes?

Hold my hand to cross the road.

Don't eat that – you might explode!

Go to bed.

Don’t suck your thumb.

I wish my goldfish was my mum.